OP
11/97

THE IRON DRAGON
❋ NEVER SLEEPS ❋

THE IRON DRAGON
❋ NEVER SLEEPS ❋

By
STEPHEN KRENSKY

Illustrated by
John Fulweiler

Delacorte ▦ **Press**

Published by
Delacorte Press
Bantam Doubleday Dell Publishing Group, Inc.
1540 Broadway
New York, New York 10036

Library of Congress Cataloging in Publication Data

Krensky, Stephen.
    The iron dragon never sleeps/by Stephen Krensky; illustrated by John Fulweiler.
        p.   cm.
    Summary: In 1867, while staying with her father in a small California mining town, ten-year-old Winnie meets a Chinese boy close to her age and discovers the role of his people in completing the transcontinental railroad.
    ISBN 0-385-31171-0
    [1. Railroads—Fiction. 2. Frontier and pioneer life—California—Fiction. 3. California—Fiction. 4. Chinese Americans—Fiction. 5. Strikes and lockouts—Fiction.] I. Fulweiler, John, ill. II. Title.
PZ7.K883Ir   1994
[Fic]—dc20   93-31167 CIP AC

Manufactured in the United States of America

May 1994

10 9 8 7 6 5 4 3 2 1

BVG

For Betty Clark

ONE

"Whooooooooo!"

Winnie Tucker jumped. The shrill blast of the train whistle had surprised her. Then she blushed. Only babies and cats were scared of train whistles.

She looked around quickly. Had anyone noticed? Her mother was reading a newspaper. The rest of the train car was mostly empty. Four men sat dozing, their heads slumped on their chests. A young woman rocked a baby in her arms.

Across the aisle, though, a man was grinning at her. He had a scraggly gray beard and a scuffed hat. Winnie's grandfathers both had looked like that. They had been miners. Maybe this man was a miner, too.

"A bit loud, eh?" he said.

1

"A little," Winnie admitted. Actually she was in awe of the train. The great locomotive up front, eating fire and breathing steam, was like an iron dragon chained to the track.

"First train ride?" the man asked.

"Uh-huh."

Her mother put down the newspaper. "The first for both of us," she said.

The man tipped his cap. "Pleased to meet you, ma'am. I'm Jack Perkins. But call me Flap Jack. Everybody does."

"Why is that?" Winnie asked.

"On account of my favorite food. After panning for gold all day, I can eat a stack a mile high."

I was right, thought Winnie. *He is a miner.*

Winnie's mother smiled. "Well, Flap Jack, I'm Marjorie Tucker. This is my daughter, Winnie. We're on our way to Cisco."

"Going to Cisco myself," said Flap Jack. "To visit my brother. He's the stationmaster there."

The train wheels squealed as the train rounded a curve. This time Winnie didn't jump.

Flap Jack looked out the window. "Making good time, I see."

Winnie pressed her nose against the glass. Flap Jack was right. The train was going fast. The trees and orchards of the California countryside were flying by. The conductor had boasted that the train

2

sometimes went as fast as twenty-five miles an hour. It was hard to believe.

Winnie and her mother had left Sacramento early that morning. Winnie's best friends, Rose and Julia, had come down to the station to say good-bye.

"Three months," Rose had moaned. "That's longer than forever."

Julia had nodded sleepily. "She will get to live in a hotel, though."

"Not a hotel," Winnie had reminded them. "A rooming house."

"Well, it won't be the same summer without you," Rose insisted.

Winnie had sighed at the time, and she sighed again now. What Rose had said was true. And she was going to miss them, she knew that.

Still, she was excited. In a few hours she'd be with her father again. She hadn't seen him in months. He was a mining engineer for the Central Pacific Railroad. It was a job that kept him on the move.

This summer, though, he was living in Cisco. At first, when her mother had suggested they come stay with him, he had been against the idea. "Cisco's no place for a girl like Winnie," he had written. Her mother had then written back: "Considering how little you've seen of her lately, how can you judge what Winnie is like these days?"

In the end he changed his mind.

Her mother patted Winnie's shoulder. "We'll be meeting Papa before you know it."

"Do you think he grew his beard again?" Winnie asked.

Her mother laughed. Eli Tucker hated to shave. His stubble was stiffer than a boar's hide, he complained. Whenever he traveled, he always managed to lose his straight-edge razor.

"Tickets! Tickets, please!"

The conductor was lurching his way up the car. He looked very grand, with his frock coat, stiff collar, and bow tie.

"Tickets?"

Winnie held hers up to the conductor.

"I've done yours already, miss," he reminded her. "One punch to a customer."

He punched a hole in Flap Jack's ticket.

"All bound for Cisco, eh?" said the conductor.

"We're going to see my father," said Winnie. "He's working on the Summit Tunnel. Maybe you know him—Eli Tucker?"

The conductor shook his head. "Those fellows don't get back here much. Digging out No. 6 keeps them pretty busy."

No. 6 was the official railroad name for the Summit Tunnel. It was part of the railroad line from Sacramento eastward through the Sierra Nevadas.

Someday the line would be part of a transcontinental railroad across the whole United States.

All the railroad tunnels were numbered in order. Winnie frowned. Numbers were so ordinary. She would have named the tunnels after book characters —like Hans Brinker or Rip Van Winkle.

The train rumbled softly.

"Are we slowing down?" Mrs. Tucker asked.

Winnie looked out again. There was no room here for a depot. They were high on the edge of a cliff.

"This is Cape Horn," said Flap Jack. "All the trains stop here for ten minutes. Gives us time to enjoy the view."

The train jolted to a halt.

"Passengers may disembark to inspect the view," the conductor announced.

Winnie was not afraid of heights. At least she didn't think she was. And if the Central Pacific Railroad thought this place was worth stopping for, she would take a look.

Cape Horn was a sheer granite bluff rising fifteen hundred feet above the American River. The train tracks ran along a ledge carved out of the mountainside. It was not very wide.

Winnie took out her sketchpad. She loved to draw, but it had been too bumpy while the train was moving.

She sketched quickly. Beyond the ledge was a steep canyon. Trees grew straight up its sides, like teeth on a comb. At the bottom was the American River. It was there, but farther downstream, where gold had been discovered in 1848.

Nineteen years had passed since then. The California gold rush was part of Winnie's family history. Her grandparents had been among the settlers flocking to California to make their fortunes. Her parents had met on a slag heap. Neither family had ever struck it rich, "but we found gold in each other," her mother liked to say.

Winnie looked up at the cliff above them. "Is this a natural ledge?" she asked.

"Not at all," said Flap Jack. "And believe me, building it was tricky work. Actually the Chinese crews did most of this. They were lowered down the side of the cliff with baskets of tools and blasting powder. They chipped out this ledge a piece at a time."

"It sounds dangerous," said Winnie.

The old miner nodded. "You could say that. Sometimes the ropes slipped. Other times the poor devils were caught too close to the exploding blasting powder. Hundreds of them lost their lives."

Winnie took a last look down. She tried to imagine herself being lowered down the cliff. Just the thought made her head spin.

"Come on, Winnie," said Mrs. Tucker. "It's time to go."

Chinese workers must be very brave, thought Winnie as she followed her mother back on board.

TWO

CISCO WASN'T SACRAMENTO. That much Winnie realized at once. There were no three-story hotels. There were no wooden sidewalks. The one wide street was lined with low buildings that looked as if they would blow over in a stiff wind.

I don't think Rose and Julia are missing much, thought Winnie. She had hoped Cisco would feel like a frontier town, a place of adventure. At first glance it just looked small.

"I don't see Papa," said Mrs. Tucker, looking from the platform to the street.

They looked inside the station. The waiting room was filled with benches and a potbellied stove. The stationmaster was just filling the oil lamps by the door.

Flap Jack sneaked up behind him.

"Bert, you old pickax!"

"Flap Jack, you old grizzly! You look as poor as ever. How was the trip?"

Flap Jack winked at Winnie. "Bert, I've ridden burros that bucked less. The ride wasn't a total loss, though. I met up with the Tuckers."

"Eli Tucker's family?" said Bert. "How do you do, ma'am? Eli told me you were coming. He should be here directly."

"I saw a general store, Mama," said Winnie. "Can we go in there while we're waiting?"

"You go ahead," said her mother. "I'll wait outside. I don't want Papa to miss us."

Winnie found the general store to be true to its name. It sold a little bit of everything. There were stores like this in Sacramento, thought Winnie, but they were bigger and had more of a selection. Here the goods were put closer together with little attention paid to the display.

Up at the counter two miners were picking out some pots and a woman was inspecting a bolt of cloth. Winnie's eyes, though, were drawn to two large jars on a nearby counter. One was filled with licorice; the other with peppermints.

Winnie walked up to the jars and tapped the glass. The peppermint was a sea of red swirls. The licorice was black.

"It is a hard choice, yes?"

On the other side of the jars stood a Chinese boy, a Celestial. Everyone called the Chinese Celestials because they called their home in China the Celestial Kingdom.

The boy was no bigger than she was, but she was tall for her ten years. Still, he looked older. She could tell that from his expression. He was wearing a blue cotton shirt, the kind all the Celestials wore. His black hair was long, and tied in the traditional pigtail. It was not hanging down his back, though, the way Chinese men wore it in San Francisco. It was coiled around his head.

Winnie had never seen a Celestial up this close before. She stared at his face, especially his eyes. They didn't really slant, she thought. They just came to more of a point at both ends.

The boy was waiting for an answer.

"Um, yes," said Winnie. "It is a hard choice. Licorice is sweet and stretchy. But peppermint tastes like winter in your mouth."

"Winter in your mouth," the boy repeated. He thought it over.

"Hey, boy! Aren't you finished yet?"

The storekeeper had come around from behind the other counter. His hands sat sharply on his hips.

"Hurry up, China boy! The railroad isn't paying you to stand around bothering my customers."

11

The Celestial bowed slightly. "I need a bowl, please. Metal. This wide." He held up his hands.

The storekeeper snorted. "You panning for gold?"

The boy shook his head. "No, no, it is for cooking."

"Oh, right . . . for that foolish peanut oil." He pointed to a far corner. "Pots and pans are over there."

Winnie took a step back. She wondered what the boy had done earlier to make the storekeeper so mad.

The storekeeper turned to her with his best smile. "He won't be bothering you anymore, miss. Now, how can I help you?"

"Um, just some licorice, thank you."

She took out her money.

"Winnie, he's coming!" her mother called from the doorway.

Winnie ran out just as Eli Tucker pulled up in a buckboard.

He turned toward the general store.

"Afternoon, ladies," he said, tipping his hat. "I do believe I've found the two prettiest women in this fair city."

He jumped down from the wagon.

"Oh, Papa," Winnie said, giggling. She ran forward to give him a hug. His beard had more gray in it than she remembered.

He returned her hug and looked up at her mother. "I'm sorry I'm late, Marjorie. It's been an upside-down day."

Winnie smiled. That was her father's way of describing a day when nothing went right.

"The powder got wet somehow," he went on. "We had to wait for some nitroglycerin. Then we had to make a new hole for the nitro. And then . . ." He smiled sheepishly. "You don't really want to hear all this, do you?"

"I'm just glad to hear your voice," said Marjorie. She came forward to join in the family hug.

Eli Tucker looked down at Winnie. "Your hair's as blond as ever. And I see you've been eating those growing pills again." He grinned. "So how was the train ride? How long did it take?"

"Only six hours. There was a lot to see."

Her father laughed. "You have to look fast when you're averaging fifteen miles an hour." He took a deep breath and looked around. "So, what do you think of Cisco?"

"I just got here, Papa." She looked around again. "But there's not much of it to think about."

Her father laughed. "You can't say I didn't warn you." He lifted the bags into the wagon. "And I haven't seen any children hereabouts. But come on, let's get you settled in. Nothing but the best for you, Winnie. Swanson's Rooming House is the finest lodging establishment in Cisco."

Marjorie laughed. "As I recall, Eli, it's the only lodging establishment in Cisco."

Her husband smiled. "Now that you mention it, that may be true."

"I'm hungry," said Winnie. She pointed to the railroad eating house beside the depot. "Are we going to eat there?"

"Certainly not!" said her father. "They charge fifty cents for a meal. Can you believe that? Only kings and presidents and folks who don't know any better eat there. For fifty cents you can eat all day at Swanson's."

On their way to the rooming house they passed a mountain mud wagon. The Chinese boy from the general store was sitting in the back. He held up some peppermints for her to see.

Winnie just looked away. If this boy was trouble, she wanted nothing to do with him.

THREE

WHEN WINNIE WOKE up the next morning, it took her a moment to remember where she was. Her room at home had flowered wallpaper and three sunny windows. This room was painted green. And the one window didn't let in much light.

There was a knock at the door.

"Come in," she called out.

Her father walked in. "Good morning," he said. "I hope you slept well." He glanced out the window. "Not much to see. There's no garden like at home."

Winnie gave him a hug. "I didn't come here for a garden, Papa. I came here for you."

He pushed a strand of hair away from her face.

"Then you should be more careful to keep this out of your eyes."

"Oh, Papa . . ."

He smiled. "So, what do you have planned for today?"

Winnie's eyes opened wide. "I'd like to go in the tunnel with you."

Her father sighed. "Now, Winnie, you know that's not possible. We can't have girls wandering around, getting in the way."

"You'd let me go if I was a boy."

"Maybe so. But you're not a boy, and that's that."

Winnie sighed.

Her father scratched his beard. "Anyway, I have a surprise for you."

Winnie perked up again. "You do? What is it?"

"If I told you, it wouldn't be a surprise. You'll find out after breakfast."

Winnie never remembered afterward whether that morning's cornmeal mush was any good. But her father made her eat it all. After she was done, he led her to the livery stable.

A horse was waiting in a stall.

"Goodness, Papa!"

"He's yours to ride while you're here. His name is Handsome. His owner says he has a high opinion of himself."

Winnie patted Handsome's mane. "Well, he should. Thank you, Papa."

Her father cleared his throat. "Remember, not too much galloping till you learn your way around. And watch out for snakes. And don't go near the tracks. The men have more than enough to do without worrying about an audience. As for the—"

"Papa, really!"

He grinned. "I guess you get the idea. Just be careful."

"Yes, Papa. I will."

Winnie and Handsome spent a lot of time exploring. In some places they found rocks jutting from the ground like the bare knuckles of a hand. In others the trees grew so close together the branches made a canopy over Winnie's head.

Toward the end of the week Winnie and Handsome came upon a crew from the railroad. Hundreds of men were filling a ravine with dirt. Some were busy shoveling. Others carted the dirt from one place to another. The faces of the men were mostly hidden under wide basket hats. Winnie knew that only the Celestials wore them.

The man in charge was a tall, bearded man bellowing out orders. He stalked up and down the line, prodding people to work faster.

The Celestials, she noticed, cringed at his approach.

Winnie noticed that several workers were not digging or carrying dirt. Instead they carried around small kegs on poles on their shoulders. They walked among the others, stopping whenever someone wanted a drink from the keg.

One of the keg carriers removed his hat briefly to wipe his forehead.

I know him, thought Winnie. It was the boy from the general store, the one who had bought the peppermints.

"Morning, miss."

One of the riding bosses had ridden up in front of her.

"Saw you up here on the ridge. Wondered what your business was."

"I—I'm Winnie Tucker. My father—Eli Tucker —works for the railroad. Maybe you know him? He warned me about getting too close, but I didn't think I was in the way up here."

The man nodded. "That's all right then. We just like to know who's keeping an eye on us."

"Everyone here seems to be working hard," said Winnie.

The man laughed. "There's no stopping these Celestials. They're just grateful, I guess."

"Grateful?"

"Sure, miss. That China they come from is a mighty poor country. So when they get here, they're happy to be alive and happy to work."

"Hennessey!"

The riding boss turned his horse. "You'll have to excuse me now. The big boss is calling." He turned his horse. "Coming, Mr. Strobridge!" he shouted, and rode back toward the tracks.

So that was Mr. Strobridge, Winnie thought. Her father had written to her about him. James H. Strobridge was the man in charge of the track construction. He and his wife lived at the railhead, the end of the tracks. Every time the tracks got longer, they moved.

Mr. Strobridge was wandering among the Celestials, cursing and encouraging them by turns. Big and tough, he was twice the size of the Chinese workers.

He looks mean, Winnie thought. Maybe it was the patch he wore over one eye. Or maybe it was just his black beard.

Handsome snorted.

"Do you smell water?" Winnie wondered.

She turned the horse toward some pines. Beyond them was a gentle slope leading down to a mountain stream.

Winnie dismounted. Handsome bent down to

drink, and Winnie did the same. The water was cool and clear.

It wasn't as warm in the shade of the pines. Winnie took out her sketchpad. She drew two squirrels playing tag in the pine needles. A rabbit sniffed at her, then hopped away before she could sketch it. A greedy chipmunk stayed longer after Winnie tossed it a biscuit she had saved from breakfast.

The chipmunk scurried away, though, as a Celestial trudged toward the stream. He was carrying two empty pails.

It's that peppermint boy again, thought Winnie.

The boy had been looking down, but he noticed her now. "I do not mean to disturb," he said. "I have come for the water."

Winnie waved at the stream. "My horse and I left you some," she said.

The boy frowned. "Left me some?"

Winnie blushed. "Never mind. It was just a joke."

"Ah." The boy nodded. "I am not always good at jokes."

Winnie smiled. "Me neither."

"We have met before, I think," said the boy. "But I did not truly introduce myself. I am Lee Cheng."

"I'm Winnie. Winnie Tucker."

"I am glad to see you again, Winnie. I have not thanked you for your wise advice."

"Advice?"

Lee smiled. "Tasting winter in your mouth."

"Oh, you mean the peppermints. That's something I used to say when I was little."

Lee wiped his forehead. "On a day like this it is nice to have winter in your mouth."

Winnie smiled.

Lee turned suddenly. Someone was yelling in the distance.

Winnie heard the words, too, but they made no sense to her. She didn't know Chinese.

Lee filled the pails quickly. "I must go," he said. "I do not want trouble."

"Like the other day," said Winnie, nodding. "That storekeeper sure was mad. What had you done anyway?"

"Done?"

"I mean, before I came in. To make him so angry."

Lee shook his head. "I had done nothing. It is just his way. I am used to it."

"I don't understand. Why—"

"I am Chinese. That is enough." Lee picked up the pails. "I must go now. I take too long for the water."

He stumbled back up the slope.

Winnie frowned. She had never thought about what being Chinese would be like. She would not have liked being yelled at just for having blond hair.

The chipmunk was chattering at her. It had come back with a friend.

"Now that I do understand," she said, and threw them another piece of biscuit.

FOUR

"Keep your voice down, Winnie," said her mother. "We're in a public place."

"All right," said Winnie. The dining room of Swanson's Rooming House didn't seem all that public to her. It held only four tables. As far as Winnie could tell, everyone who stayed at Swanson's worked for the railroad. And they were all too busy slurping their soup or talking among themselves to pay any attention to her.

Still, eating at Swanson's was very different from eating at home. For one thing, they didn't get to choose their own meals. For another thing, Papa always tucked his napkin carefully under his chin. At home he mostly used his sleeve—if Mama wasn't looking.

Tonight they were having roast beef—again. It was the third time this week.

"We have to put some meat on your bones," Mrs. Swanson had told Winnie.

Winnie was not putting much meat on her bones tonight. Her food was mostly untouched. She was thinking about Lee. Wait till Rose and Julia heard she had met a Celestial.

"Eat up, Winnie," said her mother. "Your dinner's getting cold."

Winnie took a bite of her roll.

"I met a Celestial boy today," she said. "Well, actually, I met him before. But today I talked with him. His name is Lee. Lee Cheng. He works for the railroad."

"I didn't know the railroad hired boys," said her mother. "What was he like?"

"He seemed quiet. He talked a little funny—the way he put words together. And he definitely looked funny, especially with that braid of hair on his head."

"Best place for it," said her father. "Keeps it out of the way when he's working."

Winnie hadn't thought about that. "But why have it at all?" she asked. "Why not just cut it off?"

"Can't," said her father, pouring gravy on his mashed potatoes. "From what I hear, the Manchu emperor back there in China ordered them to keep their hair that way."

"But they're in America now," said Winnie. "China is far, far away."

"Doesn't matter," said her father. "A law is a law."

Her mother sighed. "He must be a very powerful emperor," she said.

Winnie knew about emperors only from storybooks. It was hard to imagine them as real people. She couldn't really blame Lee for doing what an emperor wanted. She wouldn't want to get in trouble with an emperor either.

"What was this boy doing when you talked to him?" her mother asked.

"Getting water from a stream. He was going to refill a keg, I think. They must drink a lot of water on hot days."

Eli snorted. "It's not water they drink, it's tea. Lukewarm tea." He shuddered. "It must agree with them, though. They're never sick."

"Do you really think the tea makes them healthier?" Marjorie asked.

"Who knows?" said Eli. "Maybe it's all that cuttlefish they eat. Or the bamboo sprouts or the dried seaweed or all those vegetables. Pass the butter, please."

28

Winnie blinked. She hated vegetables. Why would anyone eat so many of them on purpose?

"Where do they get such things?" she asked.

"The Chinese foods are shipped in from San Francisco," her father explained. "Most of them arrive all dried up, like something dead or worse. After the Chinese cooks add water to the stuff, it perks up some. Not exactly like real food, though."

He shook his head and stabbed his mashed potatoes.

"What's the matter, dear?" asked Marjorie.

Eli shrugged. "Oh, it's just the tunnel. My crew spent the whole day blasting. We were trying to enlarge the heading. And how far did we get? One foot!" He slowly crushed a roll between his fingers. "Solid rock can be so—so stubborn."

"I'm sure it is, Eli," said Marjorie. "But don't take it out on the rolls."

Winnie hid a giggle in her napkin. One foot wasn't very much, though. Imagine twenty or thirty men digging only that far in a day.

"The Celestials work hard, don't they?" asked Winnie.

"Sure do," said her father. "Why, they even beat a crew of Welsh miners brought over special from Europe. I don't know where they get their energy." He sipped his coffee. "Maybe it's their baths."

Winnie looked confused. "Baths?" She disliked them almost as much as vegetables.

"Yes, baths." Her father took a bite of roast beef. "The Celestials are very organized. They've divided themselves into small groups. At night the group cook prepares a large boiler of hot water. Then the Celestials fill empty powder kegs with the water and take sponge baths."

"A bath every night?" Winnie was amazed. It sounded like torture.

"Every night," her father repeated. "Then they put on fresh clothes to eat supper."

Her mother eyed Winnie's dusty frock. "You know, Winnie," she said, "you could learn a lot from the Chinese."

Winnie wasn't so sure. Here at the rooming house there was one bathtub in a room at the end of the hall. Everyone shared it.

She sighed. Her mother was giving her that funny smile, the one she didn't really understand. Somehow Winnie had the feeling she would take more baths this summer than she ever had in her whole life.

FIVE

CISCO MAY NOT HAVE BEEN PRETTY, but it was a busy place. A train from Sacramento arrived each day. It was met there by the Overland Mail stagecoach and various freight wagons from Nevada.

Her father had told Winnie that stagecoaches would soon be a thing of the past. "The railroads will chase them into the woods," he had said. "And they won't ever come back."

Winnie wanted to get one down on paper before they disappeared. So one morning she sat down outside the general store and sketched the stagecoach across the street.

Her first picture made the wheels too big. She put it down and started another.

"I wish I could draw like that."

Winnie looked up. "Oh!" she said. "Where did you come from?"

She was speaking to a girl about her own age who was standing behind her.

"I came on that stagecoach you're drawing," the girl answered. "What's your name?"

"Winnie. Winnie Tucker."

"Nice to meet you, Winnie. I'm Jane Poole. Do you live here?"

"Just for this summer. I'm from Sacramento."

Jane sighed. It made her freckles crease. "We're moving to Portland," she said.

"Portland, Oregon?"

Jane nodded. "My father works for a lumber company there. He went on ahead two months ago. Now he's sent for us—my brother, my mother, and me. We came through Omaha from Kansas City." She closed her eyes. "That was four very bumpy weeks ago."

"My father says that once the railroad is finished, people will travel from Omaha to San Francisco in just five days."

"How does your father know that?"

"He works for the railroad company," said Winnie.

Jane nodded. "See those two men?" She pointed down the street. "I think they work for the railroad, too."

Winnie saw two strangers walking past the storage sheds of railroad supplies.

"They were with us on the stagecoach from Omaha," Jane explained. "They bragged a lot about how important they were to the railroad there—the Union Pacific."

"Hey, Jane!"

A boy was calling to her.

Jane sighed. "That's my brother, Johnny."

Johnny ran headlong into the street—and was almost hit by a passing wagon. The driver, one of the railroad cooks, yelled at him in Chinese.

Johnny yelled back.

"Did you see that?" he asked Jane. "That old man almost ran me down."

"You jumped out in front of him," said Winnie. Johnny looked a lot like his sister, but with more freckles and sandy hair. He was about eight, she reckoned.

"No, I didn't," he said. "It was all his fault. If those Chinese opened their eyes wider, they would probably see better. And they should cut their hair, too."

"They can't help their hair," said Winnie. "Their emperor makes them wear it that way."

"What emperor?"

"The one back in China." She explained about the emperor.

Johnny was not impressed. "I wouldn't let any emperor make me look like a girl." He stared at Winnie. "Who are you anyway?"

"Winnie Tucker."

"Well, what are you defending the Chinese for? You don't look Chinese."

"I'm not." Still, he was right. She had defended them. Winnie wasn't sure why. In the past she had hardly thought about the Chinese. They were just the Celestials. But Lee was a real person. He got thirsty and made jokes. He worried about getting in trouble. Meeting him made her feel a little different.

"Where's Mother?" Jane asked.

"In the general store. The train doesn't leave for a while yet. Let's play hide-and-seek." He looked at Winnie. "She can play, too."

"All right," said Winnie.

Jane smiled. "Since it was your idea, Johnny, you can be It. Count to twenty. And remember, no peeking."

"All right. One . . . two . . . three . . ."

Jane motioned for Winnie to follow her. They darted across the street and ducked behind the stagecoach.

"Quick!" Jane whispered. "Get inside."

Winnie opened the door, and they both climbed in. The stagecoach smelled of dirt and old leather.

"He'll never think to look here," Jane whispered.

"Shh. Someone's coming."

Some footsteps stopped outside.

"Did you have any luck?" said a man's hoarse voice.

Winnie pressed back against the stagecoach seat. She could see the back of a man's head outside the window.

"I talked to a few. I don't think the Chinese trusted me."

The hoarse man laughed. "I wouldn't trust you myself. You haven't changed your clothes in a week or bathed in a month." He spit on the ground. "But they've got eyes, don't they? Even if they are slanty. They see what's going on. They have to pay for their own food. They don't get promoted. And they get all the dangerous jobs to boot. I don't think they'll stand for it much longer."

"I'll drink to that. Come on. There must be some whiskey in this rathole of a town."

They walked away up the street.

"Can you believe that?" said Jane. "Imagine talking with some Chinese." She shuddered.

"I've met a Chinese boy who works for the railroad," said Winnie. "He seems nice enough."

"That's hard to believe, Winnie. I mean, they're so strange."

"How do you know if you've never talked with one?"

Jane fidgeted with her frock. "Well, I just do, that's all."

"Jane! Johnny!"

Jane sighed. "Oh-oh, that's Mother. I guess we'd better go."

They climbed out of the stagecoach.

"I'll have to help Mother find Johnny. He could be anywhere looking for us. Good-bye, Winnie. If you're ever in Portland, look for me."

"Good-bye, Jane. Hope you like the train ride!"

Winnie watched Jane and her mother head for the station. She wondered how many people thought about the Chinese the way Jane did.

"New friend?"

Winnie turned as Flap Jack came up beside her.

"Not exactly," she said. "Just someone I met. She doesn't much care for the Chinese."

"She has lots of company," said Flap Jack.

"And we heard these two men talking. They didn't like the Chinese either. But they seemed to think the Chinese are important."

"Well, they are—at least to the railroad. Bert's told me the railroad has ten thousand Celestials on the payroll."

"Well, these men were talking about the railroad

and the Celestials. They talked like the Chinese were being taken advantage of."

Flap Jack frowned. "Who were these fellows?"

"Jane said they worked for the Union Pacific."

"Hmm. That's the company building the railroad west from Omaha. They'd like to see the Central Pacific have trouble with the Chinese. Truth is, the Chinese crews are the best the railroad has."

"So if this Union Pacific caused trouble with the Chinese," said Winnie, "that would slow the Central Pacific down a bit."

"I expect so," said Flap Jack.

Winnie was confused. "But wouldn't that hurt the Union Pacific, too? I mean, wouldn't the completion of the railroad be delayed?"

"Maybe," said Flap Jack, "but it could be worth it. You see, Winnie, both companies are laying track in a kind of race. The Union Pacific is building west from Omaha. The Central Pacific is building east from Sacramento. Somewhere—in Utah or Nevada—the two railroads will meet."

Winnie shook her head. "Why does it matter where they meet? When they're done, it will still be only one railroad joined together."

Flap Jack smiled. "Ah, that's true—for the passengers. But there's more at stake than that. The government gives land to a railroad for each mile of track it lays. The more track a railroad puts down, the more land it collects. And someday that land will be worth plenty."

Winnie nodded slowly.

"Well," she said, "I guess building a railroad is more complicated than I thought."

❊ SIX ❊

On Sundays the railroad workers were supposed to rest. They caught up on their sleep or played games or even cleaned their clothes. It was the one day Winnie expected to spend with her father.

But things did not work out that way. On the first Sunday her father was in bed with a cold. On the next two, he had ended up traveling on railroad business.

The fourth Sunday, though, dawned bright and clear. It was a perfect day for a picnic. The Tuckers piled into the buckboard right after breakfast and headed for Donner Lake.

They arrived there just in time for lunch. Mrs. Swanson had made them up a basket that would have fed them twice. There was fried chicken and deviled eggs and biscuits and two kinds of pie.

Winnie tried everything, including both pies. "It's beautiful here," she said. "I wish we could stay forever."

Her mother laughed. "What about Sacramento, Winnie? Don't you want to go back?"

"Well, I miss Rose and Julia, of course." Winnie made a face. "But I'm not looking forward to school. Rose says we're going to learn to dance—"

"Dance?" Her father gasped. "How horrible! Not with boys, I hope."

Winnie folded her arms. "Not right away."

Eli smiled and mopped his brow. "That's a relief," he said.

Marjorie looked out at the lake, brushing the pie crumbs from her skirt. The blue water was still, reflecting the mountains beyond them.

"It is beautiful here," she said. "But a little sad, too."

"Sad?" said Winnie.

Her mother nodded. "The country is changing fast, Winnie. I came through here in '49 on a Conestoga wagon. It took six strong horses to pull it. The wagon was like a house on wheels. Everything we owned was in there. We lived in it for most of a year coming west from St. Louis."

"But you made it safely."

"We did. Not everyone was so lucky. Twenty

years ago people died of starvation right around here."

Winnie gulped. "Died?"

"Donner Lake is named for the Donner Party," her mother went on. "They were a group of immigrants traveling west. They got stuck up here for the winter of 1847. Many starved to death."

Even in the bright June sunshine Winnie shivered.

"Well, we won't starve," said her father, patting his stomach. "Not today at any rate." He stood up and stretched. "I have something for you in the buckboard, Winnie."

"What is it?" Winnie asked.

Her father pulled back a blanket—and took out a kite. It was shaped like a diamond with a tail of red cloth.

Winnie beamed. "It's wonderful! I'm going to try it out right now."

She ran through the field, trailing the kite behind her. She imagined the wind lifting her kite high. It would soar past the clouds. It would dance with the sun.

Winnie turned. The kite was dragging along the ground. The wind was paying it no attention at all.

"Come on, kite," said Winnie. "Do you hear me? Let's go!"

Someone laughed behind her.

Winnie turned. It was Lee Cheng, the boy from the railroad.

Winnie was embarrassed. "What are you doing here?" she demanded.

Lee shrugged. He was in a good mood. "I have cleaned my clothes. I am not needed to kill chickens and pigs. I like the lake. So here I am."

"Well, I don't need you laughing at me. Go away!"

Lee eyed the fallen kite. "I do not want to go away. I want to help."

"I know what I'm doing," said Winnie.

"A kite is like a bird," said Lee. "You cannot pull it like a wagon. May I try?"

"I guess so," said Winnie. It was hard to stay angry at someone who didn't get angry back.

She handed over the kite.

"First, we must learn the wind," he said.

Lee looped the string around his hand. Winnie had to admit he seemed to know what he was doing.

"Now we begin."

Lee ran back and forth, shifting the kite with the breeze. In his hands it truly flew like a bird. He soon had the kite up above the trees.

Winnie ran to keep up with him. "Don't you wish you could fly like that?" she asked.

"I can," said Lee, "in my dreams." He turned to Winnie. "Now it is your turn."

He gave her back the kite and showed her how to keep pressure on the string. Then they stood silently, watching the kite dip and weave against the blue sky. They stirred only when a passing cloud blocked out the sun.

"Where did you learn to fly kites?" Winnie asked.

"From my father, many years ago."

"I'm visiting my father this summer. He works for the railroad. My mother and I came out from Sacramento on the train."

"I would like to ride the train someday," said Lee. "It makes me think of a great iron dragon."

Winnie laughed. "Why, that's what I think, too. It eats fire and breathes steam."

"My brother, Tom, once rode behind the engine," said Lee. "He said it was very noisy."

"A dragon is not a quiet beast," said Winnie.

They watched the kite take a sudden dip.

"Can your parents take the train to visit you?" Winnie asked.

"No," said Lee. "They are dead. A terrible sickness took them in San Francisco. It was long ago."

"I'm sorry," said Winnie.

Lee nodded. "Afterward my brother, Tom, and I lived in a miner's house. I worked in the house. Tom worked in the mine."

"How long were you there?" Winnie asked.

"Three years. It is where I learned English. When the mine closed, we had to leave."

"Aren't you young to work for the railroad?" asked Winnie.

"They do not look at us too closely," said Lee. "And they were happy I spoke English. Tom is older. He works with miners."

"So does my father," said Winnie. "Maybe they know each other."

Lee shrugged. "There is little time for meeting," he said.

"My father's sitting over there," said Winnie. She pointed toward the water. "With my mother. Would you like to meet them? You could have some pie."

Lee looked uncomfortable. "I like pie. But I do not think so. Things are happening . . ."

"Things?" Winnie frowned. "What things?" Suddenly she remembered the two men she had overheard in town.

"Many workers are not happy. We work hard, as hard as anyone. But we are not treated the same."

Winnie thought about the storekeeper and Jane and Johnny. She didn't know what to say.

"Some voices," said Lee, "speak of working no more. They are angry voices."

"What do you think?" Winnie asked.

"I do not decide yet," said Lee. He gave her

back the kite string. "Maybe I say too much. It is getting late. Good-bye, Winnie Tucker."

He turned and ran away.

Winnie pulled in the kite and walked slowly back to her parents.

"Who was that, Winnie?" her father asked. "Chinese, wasn't he?"

"Yes, Papa. That was Lee, the Celestial I've met before."

"Lee seems to know about kites," said her mother.

Winnie nodded. "He knows a lot. He used to work for a miner—after his parents died. That's how he learned English." She paused for breath. "And, Papa, remember what I told you about those men in town? When I asked Lee about it, he got nervous. I think the Celestials are angry."

Her father sighed. "That may well be. But sometimes you can't go looking for trouble. You have to wait for it to hit you over the head. Come on now. Let's clean up. And then we'll take that boat ride I promised."

Winnie enjoyed rowing on the lake. She made ripples in the water with her hand and splashed her father with an oar. But her attention also wandered. What kind of trouble could be coming? And when? Maybe she couldn't do anything about it, but she kept thinking about Lee and the angry voices.

47

❈ SEVEN ❈

"ELI, WHAT ARE YOU DOING HERE?"

Marjorie stopped pinning for a moment. She was making a new dress for Winnie, who was standing on a stool next to her. Winnie was draped in burgundy calico.

The cloth was almost as red as her father's face. Eli Tucker looked about ready to explode.

"It's an upside-down day, Marjorie. No, worse than that. It's an inside-out day, too!"

"Can I get down, Mama?" Winnie asked. Clearly the dressmaking was going to be delayed.

"All right, Winnie. Now, Eli, calm down. Tell us what's wrong?"

"There's a strike, Marjorie. Two thousand Chinamen are on strike. Can you believe it?"

Winnie could. *This was what Lee was hinting about,* she thought.

"I mean, we expected trouble on Saturday. There were a few men holding up signs. But this morning the tunnel drillers refused to work. Mr. Strobridge must have choked on a cigar when he heard the news. And Mr. Crocker, he probably swallowed one whole."

"Mr. Crocker and the other railroad owners may be getting what they deserve," said Marjorie. "You've said the Chinese are paid twenty-six dollars a month while the others get thirty-five. And the Chinese have to pay for their own food, too."

"It's strange food, Marjorie, you have to admit that."

"Strange to us, Papa," said Winnie. "Not to them."

Her father folded his arms. "Well, that may be. But don't try to confuse the issue with facts."

"And what is the issue?" asked Marjorie.

"That strikes are not allowed. If the Chinese aren't happy here, they can leave."

"Can they?" Marjorie wasn't so sure. "I heard two men on the street bragging about the deserters they brought back to the railroad. They talked of beatings and whippings."

Her husband chewed his lip. "Some of the boys

49

may have gotten a little out of hand. That still doesn't make a strike right."

"What are the Chinese demanding?"

"They want the same pay and work hours as white workers. Mr. Crocker won't stand for it. He's coming out to take charge of the situation personally."

"Do you think there'll be trouble?" Winnie asked. "Could anyone get hurt?"

"The strike is already trouble, Winnie. If you mean dangerous trouble, I honestly don't know. So far there's been none. Most of the Chinese are holed up in the camps. They're just lying around, drinking their tea. Our orders are to leave them alone for the present."

"And if those orders change?" asked Winnie.

Her father sighed. "Then trouble will follow for sure."

Two days passed with no outward change in the situation. The Chinese stayed in their camps. There were meetings between Mr. Crocker and the strikers, but no progress was made.

"They know we need them," her father told Winnie at supper. "So they're being stubborn. But they have nowhere to go. In a way they need us, too."

"I just wish it were over," said Winnie. "Even the air feels tense."

The next morning Winnie rode Handsome out to look at the tracks. There were scattered non-Chinese crews trying to keep busy. Still, everything seemed very quiet.

The trail took her past a trestle bridge spanning a ravine. The crisscrossed wood supports rose like the top of a cherry pie on its side.

"Winnie!"

She turned in the saddle. Lee was approaching. He walked slowly, and she thought he looked tired.

"Hello, Winnie!"

Winnie dismounted. Part of her was glad to see Lee. The other part was mad at him and all the other Chinese, who were causing problems for her father.

"Why are you here?" she said. "I thought you were on strike."

"I am. That is why I can be here. There is nothing else for me to do."

"You should be working to settle this strike. You should be helping."

"I wish to help," Lee admitted. "But my words go unheard."

Winnie paused. She knew what that was like.

"My father says it's not right to strike," she said finally.

Lee sighed. "Right and wrong can be hard to tell apart. Is it right that we are up before the sun and do not rest until dark? Is it right that last winter the snow fell so deep we could not walk over it? We had to dig tunnels under the snow to go from place to place. Is it right that we had to dig holes through the snow for air?" He shivered at the memory. "The iron dragon never sleeps, Winnie. It is always waiting, always wanting more. There were some days when we didn't see the sky. But even in the tunnels we were not safe from the rumbling snows."

"Avalanches?"

Lee nodded. "One of them swept away twenty men. They were buried so deep they could not be dug out until spring."

Winnie shuddered.

"Again and again we have asked for changes. The railroad does not listen. Maybe they will listen now."

"The strike is still wrong," Winnie said softly.

Lee sighed. "Not so wrong as being buried alive in the snow."

Handsome snorted.

"He's hungry," said Winnie, glad to change the subject. "And impatient, too. I brought him a treat."

She took two apples out of her saddlebag. She offered one to Handsome, who quickly gobbled it up.

"Do you want to feed him the other?" she asked Lee.

Lee took the apple and looked at it thoughtfully. He turned it over. "It is a fine apple. Very round."

"I guess it is," said Winnie. She watched Lee closely. "Do you want to eat it?"

Lee brightened. "Yes, please."

"Go ahead. I'll get more."

Lee almost choked on the apple because he bit into it so fast.

"Slow down," said Winnie. "Why are you so hungry?"

"We have had no food since Tuesday. Mr. Crocker, the big boss, cut off our supplies."

Winnie blinked. She knew the Chinese paid for their own food. It wasn't fair for Mr. Crocker to starve them into working for him. That made him nothing more than a bully.

Winnie didn't like bullies.

"I should go," she said. "I promised to meet my mother." She chewed her lip. "Lee, do you see those pines by the ridge? Meet me there tomorrow morning. Early."

"What plan is in your head, Winnie Tucker?"

"Just be there," she said. "Please."

EIGHT

THE NEXT MORNING found Eli Tucker prowling around his room. Marjorie watched him from a chair by the window.

"Eli, you're as itchy as a bear in a briar patch."

"I can't help myself. It's this strike, Marjorie. I hate feeling like my hands are tied."

"Do you think it will last much longer?"

Eli shrugged. "The Celestials want more money and a shorter workday. I doubt they'll get much. Maybe Crocker will throw them a bone."

"What do you think they'll do?" asked Marjorie.

"They're caught betwixt and between," Eli admitted. "Poor devils. I don't know that they have much choice."

He looked under a pillow. "Where are those muffins?" he muttered.

"Muffins?" said Marjorie.

"Yes, muffins," he repeated. "Mrs. Swanson gave me a few yesterday. They were wrapped in a napkin."

"I think Winnie has them. She went out for a ride."

He frowned. "You say she took all the muffins?"

"She's a growing girl. Besides, you had breakfast. Tell me, Eli, is it true that Mr. Crocker has cut off the Chinese food supplies?"

"Where'd you hear that?"

"Cisco has big ears for such a small town. Is it true?"

He nodded. "Nothing to do with me, of course, but nothing I can do about it either. I don't approve, though, if that's what you're wondering." He cleared his throat. "Where did Winnie go anyway?"

"She went riding on Handsome."

"This early? Well, I hope she's got sense enough to stay away from the tracks. Tempers are getting short. No telling what might happen."

At the moment nothing was happening to Winnie. She was sitting under a tree by the trestle bridge. The sun was rising in the sky, and Lee was nowhere in sight.

Winnie yawned. She had not slept well. Some new men had come in late. They tromped up the stairs, laughing and talking. She could hear them as they passed by in the hall.

"They think they can wait us out," said one.

"We'll teach them a lesson," said another. "A few cracked heads is something they'll understand."

Winnie sighed and took out her sketchpad. Us and Them. Was this some kind of game? Was she supposed to be on the railroad's side because of her father? Or just because she wasn't Chinese?

"Over here, Lee!" she shouted as he appeared on the ridge.

Lee came forward slowly. Twice he looked back over his shoulder.

"I am sorry to be late. There was a meeting. I wanted to hear what was said. This Mr. Crocker is a hard man. He has spoken very plain. If we do not return to work by Monday, he will act."

Winnie nodded. "I know. My father says Crocker will fine you for keeping his other men and equipment idle." She paused. "He's used to getting his way, I think. Well, let's not talk about *that* for now. I brought you some muffins. And more apples. And a sandwich, too. Mrs. Swanson made it for me."

She indicated the sack at her side.

"Help yourself."

Lee examined the contents.

"There is too much here," he protested. "You will eat, too?"

"Oh, I had a big breakfast," Winnie lied. "You go ahead."

Lee bit into a corn muffin. "Very good," he said.

Winnie looked relieved. "I didn't know what you liked," she admitted.

"I like salted cabbage, dried seaweed, bamboo sprouts, and mushrooms," said Lee.

"We didn't have any vegetables or cuttlefish. I don't like vegetables much."

"The way Americans cook them, I would not like them either. But I eat other things, too."

He turned his head. "Did you hear that?"

"Hear what?"

Lee frowned. "Perhaps it is nothing. But three men were walking not far behind me. They moved as I moved. And they were carrying clubs."

"Oh."

"I tried to run ahead and hide my way. I do not know if I succeeded."

"I don't hear anything now," said Winnie. "You said you went to a meeting this morning. Did it go well?"

"Not so good, I think. Many workers are angry. They came to this country to make money. It is money they want to take home."

"Home?" Winnie was surprised. "You mean back to China?"

Lee nodded. "Most who come do not wish to stay. The ones who do not gamble can save twenty dollars a month. That is a lot of money in China. My father always planned to return home to Kwangtung Province and buy a farm."

Winnie could not imagine leaving her own country just to find work. And then to go back afterward! The Chinese must love their country very much to do that.

"And your mother came with him?" she asked.

"No, no," said Lee. "It is not a trip for women. He met my mother here, in San Francisco."

All the time Lee had been talking, Winnie had been sketching. She always had trouble doing people because they moved too much. But Lee remained still while he spoke.

"What are you doing?" he asked.

Winnie blushed. "Just drawing."

Lee got up to take a look. "That is me!" he cried. He touched the paper gently.

"I'm glad you think so," said Winnie. "Would you like to have it?"

Lee looked surprised. "To keep? It would be a special gift." He paused. "I do not have anything for you in return."

"That's all right. I like to give away my drawings."

They both heard the twigs crack.

"Quick!" whispered Winnie. "Behind the trestles."

"What about you?" whispered Lee.

"Don't worry," she said. "It's not me they want."

Winnie started sketching quickly as three men came over the ridge. They stopped at the sight of her.

"Hey! What are you doing there?"

"Just drawing," said Winnie. She held up her drawing paper. "Why, is something wrong?"

"We were following one of those Chinese boys. He got loose from their camp."

"Yeah," said another, shouldering his club. "We wanted to make sure he didn't get into any trouble."

Winnie recognized their voices. These were the men she had heard on the stairway.

"You seen anyone hereabouts?"

Winnie scratched her head. "I did hear a noise— off to the left there."

"Much obliged," said the third man, tipping his hat. "If you see anyone, though, just holler."

They turned off the path and scrambled down the hill.

Winnie waited two full minutes, barely daring to breathe. Then she walked up to the ridge for a look.

"They're gone now," she said.

Lee emerged from the shadows. He brushed the dirt from his pants.

"I owe you much," he said.

"Let's call it even," said Winnie. "After all, I'm the reason you're here in the first place." She let out a long breath. "But maybe we should be going. If you like, we could meet somewhere else tomorrow. Maybe closer to your camp."

Lee sighed. "I do not think so," he said. "It could be dangerous for you." He grinned abruptly. "And for me, too. But thank you, Winnie Tucker. This is a morning I will not forget."

❊ NINE ❊

EARLY MONDAY MORNING the Celestials all returned to work. The strike had lasted only a week. But it had been seven long days for everyone concerned.

As Eli Tucker had predicted, few of the Chinese demands were met. They received another two dollars a month for their trouble, but nothing else changed.

The weeks passed quickly after the strike was settled. On some mornings Winnie found ice already creeping around the edge of the snow ponds. And the squirrels began to gather nuts constantly, except when afternoon rains pelted the ground like hail.

Winnie saw even less of her father than before. He was almost always busy. The strike had cost the railroad time. The loss was a luxury they could not afford.

"We're cutting a fair number of corners," Eli remarked more than once at dinner.

"You must be careful," said Marjorie.

"Is it dangerous digging in the tunnel?" Winnie asked.

Her father paused. "The railroad doesn't think so," he said, and was silent after that.

One late afternoon Winnie and her mother went to pick up her father on the mountain. The buckboard clattered along the bumpy dirt road. The ride rattled Winnie's teeth.

"I wish Papa didn't work late so often," she said.

"It's not his choice," said her mother. "The railroad's in an awful hurry."

"I know, I know. I don't think the Celestials even get time to breathe."

"How is Lee, by the way?" asked her mother. "Eating better, I hope."

Winnie glanced at her mother, but she kept her face forward.

"I haven't talked to him lately," said Winnie. "I've seen him passing at times. He always looks tired." She paused. "Isn't that Flap Jack over there?"

It was. The old miner waved to them from the far side of a meadow.

They stopped the wagon.

Flap Jack hobbled over. "I twisted my ankle," he said. "Stepped in a gopher hole."

"What are you doing up here?" Winnie asked.

"Sometimes even Cisco seems a bit crowded," he replied. "I was getting some air."

"We can give you a ride back to town," said Marjorie. "But first we have to pick up Eli."

"I'm a rich man where time is concerned," said Flap Jack. "As long as I can sit down, I'll be fine."

Winnie moved into the back of the wagon to make room for Flap Jack up front. He settled in, and they continued on their way.

Their route followed the train tracks heading for Donner Lake. Much of the track was not visible, though. It was covered by half-completed wooden sheds.

"Look how they're covering up the tracks," said Winnie. "I wonder why."

Her mother smiled. "Those are snowsheds."

"Snowsheds?"

"To keep the track from getting covered with snow in the winter."

"Can't they just plow the snow off?" Winnie asked.

Her mother shook her head. "Not always. Last winter, your father told me, it took five locomotives to push one plow through a fifteen-foot drift. And even at that, the plow couldn't always get through. So the railroad is building these snowsheds to keep the tracks clear."

"Look!" cried Flap Jack.

They could see fire and smoke rising from the mountain ahead.

"It's like a volcano," said Winnie. She had never seen one in person, but she had seen pictures in a book.

Mrs. Tucker pulled the buggy to a halt. Thunderous explosions were shaking the air. Tons of rocks and dirt were shooting skyward. The sound echoed down the canyons like a string of firecrackers.

"What's going on?" asked Mrs. Tucker.

"They're hurrying the blasts in before sunset," said Flap Jack.

"Whoa!" said Mrs. Tucker, steadying their horse.

Suddenly the blasts stopped.

Flap Jack frowned. "Now that's odd," he said. "They don't usually stop all at once like that. Generally one spot or another needs clearing up. Unless . . ."

"Unless what?" asked Winnie.

Flap Jack didn't answer.

"Someone's coming," said Winnie.

"And fast," said her mother.

A moment later a rider came cantering around the bend.

"What's wrong?" Flap Jack shouted.

"Been an accident," said the rider as he went by. "Got to fetch the doctor."

And then he was gone.

Winnie and her mother shared a worried glance.

"Giddyup there," said Marjorie.

TEN

THE FIRST THING THEY SAW was the collapsed tunnel entrance. Where a large hole had stood minutes before, there was now only a jumble of rocks and dirt.

The air hung heavily with dust. Most of the shouting had stopped, but the foremen were still trying to organize the crews into long lines.

One foreman saw the Tuckers pull up in the buggy. He rushed over to them.

"Mrs. Tucker?"

"Yes."

"How did you get here so soon?"

She looked confused. "I don't understand."

"I mean, it's only been minutes. How did you know that Eli—"

He stopped abruptly, seeing the change in her expression.

"I didn't know," she said slowly. She pointed to the tunnel. "Eli? Eli's trapped in there?"

"He came over this afternoon," said the foreman. "We needed his help."

"What happened?" asked Flap Jack.

"Someone set a charge too close to the support beams. The explosion knocked several of them out. Some men are trapped inside. About eight, I think." He gulped. "But don't you worry, we'll get Eli out. We'll get them all out."

Marjorie nodded dully.

Winnie looked at the huge pile of rubble. The crews were digging frantically at it, but they didn't seem to be making much of a dent.

Winnie felt dizzy. Her father was trapped behind that small mountain. She wanted to be brave, but she only felt frozen. It was easy to read about courage in a book. It was different when it was really happening.

"Step aside! Make room!"

It was Mr. Strobridge. His beard looked even darker in the lengthening shadows.

Winnie was glad to see him. He was in charge, wasn't he? He was sure to do something.

He started by shouting orders. Some men

brought up more pickaxes and shovels. Others tied ropes around some of the fallen timbers.

Come on, thought Winnie. *Faster! Faster!*

"What's going on?" her mother asked. "It looks as if some things are being done twice. Why isn't everyone working together?"

"White crews won't work with the Celestials," Flap Jack explained.

"Why not?" asked Winnie.

The old miner sighed. "Because they're Chinese. That's all the reason they need. White workers are willing to boss the Celestials, but they won't work as a team."

But this is an emergency, thought Winnie.

Winnie looked around anxiously. It was then she saw Lee standing quietly beside her.

"Oh!"

"I am sorry, Winnie Tucker. I did not mean to frighten you."

You look pretty frightened yourself, thought Winnie. Then she remembered what the foreman had said. Eight or nine men were trapped in the tunnel. Was one of them Lee's brother?

"My father is in there," she said quietly.

"And Tom," said Lee.

What if they never get out? thought Winnie. *What if they're already—*

"Listen up, men!" Mr. Strobridge called out.

"Digging will take hours or even days. We have neither. We may not even have minutes. Who knows how much air they have?" He sighed. "We'll have to risk blasting."

"That might just seal them in," said a foreman.

Mr. Strobridge tugged on his beard. "It might. Or it might blow them to kingdom come. But what other choice is there?"

No one answered him.

"Bring on the nitroglycerin," he ordered.

Workers carefully carried the explosive from the back of a nearby wagon.

Flap Jack whistled softly. "That's tricky stuff," he whispered. "A lot more powerful than gunpowder."

The miners carefully put down the explosive. Winnie watched them closely. They seemed very calm as they dug holes for their charges. The nitroglycerin itself was an oily yellow liquid. It did not look like much.

"Hold on, Papa," she whispered. "Hold on."

When the miners finished, they lit the fuses. Everyone ducked for cover.

The explosion rocked the canyon. Winnie had covered her ears, but they still ached from the sound.

Marjorie Tucker peered through the dust. "How long?" she whispered.

The crews were scrambling up the rubble.

"They cleared away a good bit with that first blast," said Flap Jack. "Now they'll—"

Suddenly another explosion rocked the landscape. Three men were tossed into the air. They landed hard and didn't move.

"Confound it!" Mr. Strobridge shouted. "I'll have Howden's hide!"

"Who's Howden?" Winnie asked.

Flap Jack brushed the dust from his coat. "He makes the nitroglycerin for the railroad. But blaming him for the explosion is like blaming the candy maker for giving you a toothache."

"What went wrong?" asked Marjorie.

"One charge did not explode on time," said Lee. "We use nitroglycerin to bite the mountain. Sometimes it bites us back."

"The fuse may have been set wrong," said Flap Jack. "Until somebody jarred it."

Other workers stepped forward cautiously with stretchers for the injured men.

"I don't see anything," said Marjorie.

Flap Jack squinted through the dust. "That first blast just got things started," he said. "Now they'll dig for a while before blasting again."

Lee was wringing his hands. He wanted to help, but the foremen had already shooed him away twice.

Winnie looked down. Her own hands were shaking.

"I hate all this waiting," she said.

"Waiting is hard," said Lee. "It is a thing my father talked much about. The worst waiting for him came on his trip to America. The ship was so full the men could barely lie down. There was fighting over food and space. There was much sickness everywhere.

"But worst of all, he said, was the waiting. Days and days and more days to come. Men died all around him. The smell was terrible. The food was so bad he closed his eyes while he ate. Still, there was more waiting.

"He wondered if he had made a good choice. He had been poor in China, but China was home. Leaving had been hard. This voyage was harder.

"Finally he reached San Francisco. So much remained unknown, but at least the waiting was over. He would never forget it, he said."

It took an hour of digging before they were ready to blast again.

It's an upside-down day for sure, Papa, thought Winnie. *But it's not over yet.*

As the fuses were lit again, Winnie squeezed her eyes shut and looked away.

The next explosion peppered everyone with pebbles and dirt. When the dust cleared, there was a small opening into the tunnel. Two crews rushed forward and enlarged the hole.

"We've found them," they called out.

Everyone hushed, waiting for news from inside the tunnel.

"And they're all alive!"

"Hooray!" shouted Winnie. She felt happy and excited and relieved all at once. She gave her mother a big hug. Then she hugged Flap Jack. And then she hugged Lee.

He even hugged her back.

Then they realized they were hugging—and quickly jumped apart.

The crews stepped aside as the miners emerged from the tunnel hole. One was limping. Another was favoring an arm. Several were carried out on stretchers.

"Tom! Tom!"

Lee rushed to the side of a man on a stretcher. He was so covered in dirt that Winnie couldn't get a good look at him.

"Eli!"

"Papa!"

Her father was being helped out of the tunnel. "Careful there," he said as they rushed forward. "I think I busted something."

The next few minutes were filled with hugs and

kisses. Before they were done, it was hard to tell who was wearing the most dirt.

Winnie had tried to say something, but the words kept getting stuck in her throat. But now she looked at her father, covered in smudges and grit—and she laughed.

"I think you're going to need a bath," she said.

Eli Tucker smiled—and then clutched his side. "I think we all will," he said, wincing.

For once Winnie didn't mind the idea of a bath at all.

ELEVEN

WHAT WINNIE ALWAYS REMEMBERED afterward was
the doctor's office. It had a few chairs, a table, and a
sink in the corner. There was an imposing cabinet
with a glass front. It had bottles inside. Winnie
couldn't read the labels.

The room had a funny smell. It made Winnie
glad she hardly ever got sick.

Still, she was happy to go there with her father.
She had to wait while the doctor changed his bandages, but she didn't mind. He was going to be all
right soon enough.

One time Winnie asked the doctor about Lee's
brother, Tom.

"Tom?" the doctor had replied. "Tom who?"

"Tom Cheng."

"Oh, one of the Celestials." The doctor shrugged. "Did he die?"

"Well, no." Winnie had once seen the bodies of two Chinese workers who had died. They had been laid out and covered with a rice mat.

"Then he's probably all right."

"Well, how was he when you saw him?"

"Me? I didn't examine him."

"But he was in the tunnel with my father. He was carried out on a stretcher."

"Yes, yes." The doctor was unconcerned. "I'm sure he was. But I don't treat Celestials."

Winnie frowned. "Why not? They work for the railroad, too."

The doctor shrugged. "It's just company policy. The Celestials have their own ways and medicines. I'm sure he's doing fine."

Winnie wasn't satisfied. She later asked her father about it. What was the railroad doing for the injured Chinese workers?

"I don't know, Winnie. You heard the doctor. They have their own ways. Probably something to do with vegetables."

Winnie might have smiled at that when the summer began. She wasn't smiling now.

"But they were hurt as much as you. Doesn't the railroad care?"

"The railroad"—Eli sighed—"has a lot of things

79

on its mind." He looked at her a little sadly. "I'm tired, Winnie. We'll talk about it another time."

Her father was tired a lot that first week. But soon he was up and around again.

"The way Mrs. Swanson is feeding me," he said ten days after the accident, "my ribs are going to have to grow back bigger just to fit my stomach." He patted his side. The strips of cloth were wrapped around his chest and stomach. "These bandages sure feel tight."

Marjorie allowed herself a smile. "It's like a corset," she commented.

"I suppose so. I don't know how women breathe in those things," he said.

"They don't," she replied. She looked into her sewing basket. "Winnie, I'm out of red thread. Run down to the store and buy another spool. I want to finish your dress before we leave."

The general store had changed little over the summer. Except for the appearance of a few winter goods, this could have been the day she arrived.

The candy was still in the same place, too.

"Try the peppermints," said a voice behind her. "It tastes like winter in your mouth."

It was Lee who had spoken.

"How are you?" said Winnie. She knew his face well from drawing the portrait. He looked a little thinner.

"I am well."

"And how is your brother?"

"He is better. Already back to work."

"But he must need time to—"

"No work, no pay," Lee explained. "Railroad always in a hurry. Summer is ending."

"I know," said Winnie. "I'm going home in a few days."

Lee nodded. "You return to the house with the garden."

"Yes. And school . . ." She made a face.

"I have always wondered about school," said Lee. "I have never been."

"You're lucky."

"Perhaps. I do not always feel lucky."

"My father says the railroad will be done in another year or two. What will you do then?"

"There will be railroads to build for many years. I cannot think more than that."

"Hey!" cried the storekeeper. He stepped in front of Winnie and stared down at Lee. "I've warned you before. Stop bothering my customers."

"I meant no—" Lee began.

"Excuse me," said Winnie, tugging on the storekeeper's sleeve. "He wasn't bothering me." She took a deep breath. "And as near as I can tell, he wasn't bothering you or anyone else either."

"Now, see here, young lady—"

"Don't worry," she said, deciding the spool would have to wait. "There won't be any trouble. My friend Lee and I were just leaving."

The storekeeper stood there gaping while Winnie and Lee walked out the door together.

TWELVE

THE TRAIN WHISTLE BLEW ONCE.

Eli Tucker was helping Marjorie and Winnie up onto the train. Their luggage was already on board.

"Time to go," said Eli. He gave Winnie a kiss. "You take care of your mother, all right?"

Winnie nodded. It was hard to believe she was going home. Rose and Julia were waiting. It would be good to see them. Still, her railroad summer had passed all too quickly.

"Cheer up, Winnie! You'll like school, I'm sure."

"Take care, Marjorie. I'll see you in a few weeks."

"Don't forget to shave, Papa!"

Her father cupped his hand to his ear. "What's

that?" he asked, smiling. "It's hard to hear over the engine noise."

"Never mind," said Winnie. "Just be careful."

The train shuddered.

"Let's go sit down," said Mrs. Tucker.

"I think I'll watch from here," said Winnie. "I'll come in after we leave."

"All right, dear. But just for a minute."

The train started up.

Winnie took a last look at Cisco. The row of low buildings hadn't changed much during her stay. And soon the railroad would be moving its supplies.

"To the other side of the mountains," her father had said.

Farther and farther, she thought. *And with so many miles to go.*

Wasn't that someone coming down the street? It looked like Lee. What was he carrying?

He seemed to be running for the train.

"Wait! Wait!" he cried.

The train was still moving slowly, slowly enough that Lee could catch it.

"What are you doing?" Winnie shouted.

"I have brought you something," he shouted back.

He ran alongside the train car and handed her a package.

"A farewell gift," he said. Then he fell back, panting for breath.

Winnie unwrapped the gift.

It was a kite made of red paper and wood, a kite shaped like a dragon.

"Thank you, Lee," she called out. "It's beautiful."

He nodded and waved good-bye.

Winnie waved, too. As the train gained speed, she tied the string to the railing and released the kite behind the platform.

The red dragon twisted and turned in the rippling wind. Then its wings steadied, and it rose high into the air. There it stayed, the paper dragon above the iron one, proudly flying over the train tracks that ran west to the mountains and east to the sea.

✺ AFTERWORD ✺

THE IRON DRAGON NEVER SLEEPS is a story set during the construction of the transcontinental railroad. Almost all the characters are fictional. The major places and events, though, are true. The town of Cisco was a staging point for the Summit Tunnel construction in 1867. It was the only time during those years that a mining engineer like Eli Tucker might have stayed in one place long enough for his family to come live with him.

For many years building a transcontinental railroad had been considered impossible. There were problems of transporting supplies. There were problems of assembling a work force. Most of all, there was the problem of crossing the Sierra Nevadas.

In the late 1850s, though, an engineer named

Theodore Judah surveyed a route through the Sierra Nevadas. Largely forgotten today, Judah laid the groundwork for the huge project that followed.

This project required thousands of workers, and the Central Pacific Railroad quickly ran short of men. It was Charles Crocker who suggested trying out the Chinese. He was one of the Central Pacific's four owners. The other three were Mark Hopkins, Leland Stanford, and Collis Huntington. They provided the money and political connections the railroad needed.

Crocker himself oversaw the construction process. By 1867 Chinese immigrants made up much of his work force. They were paid less and treated more harshly than other workers. In protest the Chinese actually went on strike. This strike, in June 1867, ended a week later under the threat of heavy punishment.

Crocker and the track supervisor, James Strobridge, did not take criticism well. They never admitted taking advantage of the Chinese. Instead Crocker claimed (without proof) that agents of the Union Pacific Railroad had encouraged the strike. Crocker respected the Chinese at work, but he did not respect them in other ways.

He shared this attitude with most of his countrymen. Chinese immigrants received little credit for building the railroad. Contemporary reports were quick to mention their unusual (for the time) taste in food or bathing habits. Yet their dedication and hard work went unmentioned.

The transcontinental railroad was finally completed on May 10, 1869. A gold rail spike was used to mark the final connection. Afterward officials of both the Central Pacific Railroad and the Union Pacific Railroad gave speeches. They were grateful for having reached such a milestone. They thanked themselves, and they thanked each other. They thanked God, and they thanked the United States government.

Nobody thanked the Chinese. Yet without their contribution—their energy, their reliability, their willingness to undertake dangerous and thankless tasks—driving in that golden spike would have been delayed for many years.